The Pet Patrol 1: Puppy Love

Betsy Duffey was born in South Carolina in the United States of America. She is the daughter of the acclaimed children's writer, Betsy Byars. Betsy Duffey has written a number of books for children, and currently lives in Atlanta, Georgia, with her husband and two sons.

Betsy Duffey

THE PET PATROL 1

PUPPY LOVE

Illustrated by Kay Hodges

PUFFIN BOOKS

PUFFIN BOOKS

Published by the Penguin Group
Penguin Books Ltd, 27 Wrights Lane, London w8 5TZ, England
Penguin Books USA Inc., 375 Hudson Street, New York, New York 10014, USA
Penguin Books Australia Ltd, Ringwood, Victoria, Australia
Penguin Books Canada Ltd, 10 Alcorn Avenue, Toronto, Ontario, Canada M4V 3B2
Penguin Books (NZ) Ltd, 182–190 Wairau Road, Auckland 10, New Zealand

Penguin Books Ltd, Registered Offices: Harmondsworth, Middlesex, England

First published in the United States by Viking 1993
First published in Great Britain by Puffin Books 1994
3 5 7 9 10 8 6 4 2

Text copyright © Betsy Duffey, 1993
Illustrations copyright © Kay Hodges, 1994
All rights reserved

The moral right of the author has been asserted

Filmset by Datix International Limited, Bungay, Suffolk
Printed in England by Clays Ltd, St Ives plc
Set in 12/15 pt Monophoto Garamond

To Danielle, Ryan,
and Elinor
– B.D.

Contents

Up, Up, and Away

"Now?" Evie called out. "Now?"

She held the bunch of balloons high in the air. They tugged upward, making Evie feel like she could almost fly up with them. She bounced a few times on the soles of her tennis shoes.

"Now?" she asked Megan again.

"No," called Megan. "Wait for the wind."

Evie and Megan stood looking up at the ten bright orange balloons standing out boldly against the summer sky. Under each balloon fluttered a white slip of paper. On each slip of paper was a message.

The girls stood on the highest point in Douglasville, the crest of Cooley's Knob. The woods stretched behind them; the cliff dropped off in front.

Evie felt a small breeze blowing down from the mountains to the north. She shivered a little.

"It'll never work," said Megan. She looked up at the balloons. "'Towns make up only a

small portion of Douglasville County. Most of the county is fields and farmland. Chances are slim that a balloon will land where people will get it."

Evie frowned at Megan. "You sound like an encyclopaedia." She was determined not to let Megan spoil her fun. "It will work."

In her mind Evie could already see the balloons floating up, up on their way to other places, other towns. The start of the journey for the balloons, the start of business number six for the girls!

"And another thing," Megan continued. "How many people out there have problems that would make them need *us*? How many would even try a couple of kids? How many —"

"Now?" Evie asked again. It was easy to ignore Megan today. Evie didn't want to think about failure. She didn't want to be reminded of their five failed businesses. To Evie the start of a new business was always a fresh start.

Megan sighed.

"We should have asked Tiffie Sullivan to get her dad to put an ad in the newspaper," she said. "Tiffie's dad *owns* the paper. He could —"

"Tiffie Sullivan!" said Evie. Megan finally had

her full attention. "I don't want to hear another word about Tiffie Sullivan. We do not need Tiffie Sullivan."

Tiffie was in their class at school. She lived in a big house in a new neighbourhood near theirs. One day she had ridden to school in a limousine.

Show-off, Evie had thought.

Tiffie wore designer clothes to school every day. Evie never wore anything but jeans. She ran her free hand over the softness of the worn denim. Let Tiffie keep her expensive clothes. But . . .

One time last year, Megan had spent the night with Tiffie. She still talked about Tiffie's perfect pink-and-white room with the pink-and-white lace bedspread and pink-and-white curtains. There was a real canopy covered in white lace over the bed. Tiffie's mother would not let anything in the room that was not pink or white. She had ordered everything from a catalogue.

An old patchwork quilt was Evie's bedspread. It had not been ordered. Her grandmother had made it from Evie's baby clothes. In the quilt were squares of cloth with faded ducks, bunnies, and teddy bears. One square was a piece of Evie's favourite baby blanket, the one that she had been wrapped in when her parents brought her home from the hospital. One square had the pocket from her first tiny dungarees. Evie would rather have her quilt than any fancy lace bedspread. But . . .

Megan seemed to think Tiffie was wonderful. Worst of all, Tiffie was having a birthday party this afternoon. The girls who were invited were going to have their own fashion show. Tiffie's father was going to take pictures for the newspaper. Megan had been invited. Evie had not. She did not even like fashion shows. She didn't mind. Not at all. But . . .

Evie looked up at the balloons and then over at Megan. Megan was smart. Megan was sensible. But this time Megan was wrong.

They didn't need an ad in the newspaper. They didn't need Tiffie Sullivan. The balloons *would* work. She just knew it.

"Now?" she asked again. "Should I let them go now?" She hopped on one foot and then the other. With her free hand she brushed her hair back from her face.

"Let's check the wind," called Megan. She put her finger in her mouth to wet it, then held it up high. With her free hand Evie did the same.

On one side of her finger Evie could feel the cool wind blowing away from the mountains north of town, blowing south towards the town of Douglasville, south onwards to Minnistron, Six Mile, and Grumptown. Out to where someone might need them.

"It's blowing south!" Evie called out.

"It's time!" yelled Megan, finally caught up in the excitement.

"Now?" asked Evie.

"Now!" answered Megan.

Evie let go of the balloons. At first they floated up as a bunch. Then they hit the wind and began to drift apart.

The sight reminded Evie of a giant orange space station sending out messenger spaceships to all the different planets. One by one each balloon took its own path.

The girls watched the balloons until they were tiny specks in the sky. They kept watching until the specks disappeared.

"It'll be great!" Evie said softly.

"It probably won't work," said Megan.

They took one more look at the sky and turned to walk back down the mountain.

"It *will* work," said Evie. "Just wait. You'll see."

She thought of the white slips of paper on the balloons. She smiled a little as she thought about their message.

Have a lost pet? . . . We'll find it!
Have a lonely pet? . . . We'll mind it!
Have a bad pet? . . . We'll teach it!
Have a trapped pet? . . . We'll reach it!
Have a hungry pet? . . . We'll feed it!
The Pet Patrol? . . . You'll need it!

The Pet Patrol
4591 Carter's Mill Road
Call us: 555-9001

The Pet Patrol was now in business. And this was one business that was going to work!

Maybe, Maybe Not

"We're in business!" said Evie.

The girls were walking down the path towards town.

"We're in business," said Megan, "*if* it works."

"It will work," said Evie. "Just wait."

"That's what you said about business number two," said Megan.

Evie was quiet now. Megan was still sensitive about the trumpet idea.

The idea had been a good one. Evie had decided that they would charge fifty pence for a song on Megan's new trumpet.

'It'll be great!" Evie had said.

It hadn't been great.

Megan got out her trumpet. They'd stopped at each house on Carter's Mill Road. At each house Megan played one song.

At the first house Megan put the trumpet to her mouth and . . .

Hiss hiss honk!

Evie hadn't been able to tell what song it was. After the first song, they got the feeling that the neighbours were paying them to stop playing the song.

They made three pounds and fifty pence before Megan's mum took the trumpet away.

Now they walked on down the path side by side. Evie cleared her throat.

"Well, let's just say it *could* work," she said.

"That's what you said about business number one."

Evie was silent again.

Megan had also been right about their weed-pulling business, five pence a weed. Another one of Evie's great ideas.

"It'll be great," Evie had said.

It hadn't been great.

Their first job had been weeding Mrs Hansen's flower beds. They had been proud of the growing pile of weeds at the end of the flower bed. Evie had counted up their earnings as they threw the weeds on to the pile.

"Twenty-five pence!"

"Fifty-five pence!"

"One pound, forty pence!"

They had pulled over fifty weeds before they found out that they were not pulling weeds, but Mrs Hansen's begonias.

Megan had called out their loss of money as they had planted each begonia back into the flower bed.

"One pound, forty."

"Fifty-five."

"Twenty-five."

Their first weed-pulling job had been their last.

Evie had had lots of other great ideas. She hoped that Megan would not bring them *all* up.

There had been business number three, the rock-selling business, and business number four, the baby-feeding business, and business number five, the car-washing business. Some of Evie's great ideas were better off forgotten.

The path ended at an earth road. Megan and Evie turned on to it and kept walking. The road looped back and forth through the trees. They were almost at the duck pond.

They always stopped to feed the ducks. On the way up to the mountain they had been carrying the balloons and couldn't stop. The ducks had

followed them half-way up the path, quacking their disappointment.

"Sorry, ducks!" Megan had called as they went by.

Evie smiled. Megan was always saying things like that. Sorry, ducks. Give it up. Don't get your hopes up. It will never work. Megan hated disappointment.

Evie pulled a small bag of old bread out of the pocket of her jacket and concentrated on the ducks.

She handed Megan an old hot-dog bun and took a stale slice of bread for herself. They pulled pieces off the bread and threw them into the water.

Quack!

The ducks raced in a group towards one piece, then another. They attacked the bread and pecked at each morsel until it was gone. Evie and Megan threw the pieces as far as they could.

"I wonder what our first job will be," Evie said. She pulled off another piece and threw it in the direction of the smallest duck.

Megan didn't answer. She was too busy quacking to the ducks. But Evie's eyes grew brighter as she thought about the animals they could help.

"There you are, ma'am," she would say as she climbed down from a tree with a fuzzy kitten she had rescued.

"Here you go, sir," she would say as she returned a lonely lost dog to its owner.

At last they had found the perfect business. No one loved animals as much as Evie and Megan.

"Evie?"

She looked up. Megan was holding out her hand for more bread. Evie pulled the last hot-dog bun out of the bag.

While Megan tore up the bun and threw it to the ducks, Evie tipped the crumbs out of the bag and stuffed the empty bag back into her pocket.

Quack!

The ducks circled and demanded more.

"Sorry, ducks," said Megan. She lifted up her hands to show that they were empty. "All out."

Evie smiled.

"See you next time," she said to the ducks.

The girls walked back to the road and turned towards home.

Evie looked at her watch. "By *now*," she said, "we really *could* have business!"

Megan just shook her head.

"Well, it wouldn't hurt to go to my house and check the answering machine," Evie said. "It's been over an hour now since we let the balloons go."

"It may still be too early," said Megan, but she went along anyway.

The earth road turned into a paved road and the woods turned into a neighbourhood. They cut across Mr Shiver's garden and climbed over Mrs Hansen's back fence.

Then they headed down Carter's Mill Road towards Evie's house.

"We *could* have business," Evie said again. "When we get there, someone could be waiting for us." Evie began to walk a little faster.

"Don't get your hopes up," said Megan, but she began to walk a little faster, too.

"Maybe," said Evie.

"Maybe not!" said Megan.

"Come on!" said Evie. They broke into a run.

As they ran down the last part of Carter's Mill Road, Megan and Evie yelled back and forth.

"Maybe!"

"Maybe not!"

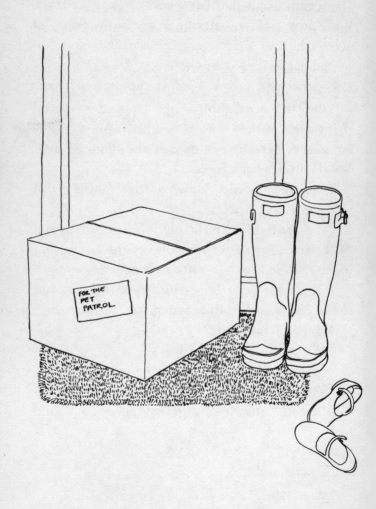

"Maybe!"

"Mayb—"

Megan stopped. She wasn't yelling "Maybe not" now. She was staring at the front porch of Evie's house. Evie stopped beside her and followed her gaze to the porch.

Neither girl said a word as they stared at the porch. There was no arguing now.

On the front porch was a big cardboard box. On the side of the box, in bold black marker, were four words:

FOR THE PET PATROL.

Puppies!

Yap! Yap!

Sounds were coming from the box. Sounds that told the girls exactly what kind of animals were inside.

"Puppies!" they yelled together as they ran towards the porch.

They ripped off the masking tape that was holding the box loosely closed. Four puppies jumped up and down against the sides.

"Puppies!" said Evie again as she picked up a wiggling ball of brown-and-white fur.

"Puppies!" said Megan as she picked up two furry golden ones.

They looked down at the box. One small black puppy was left.

Yap!

He barked impatiently. He stood on his back legs waiting to be lifted up with the others. He was smaller than the rest and not as furry.

Megan and Evie laughed.

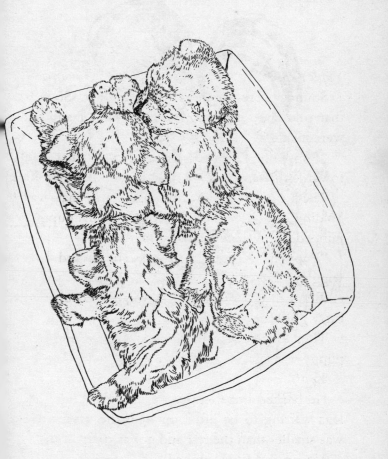

"You must be the runt!" said Evie. She adjusted the brown-and-white puppy in one arm and picked up the black puppy.

As she reached down she saw a note. It was taped to the inside of the box. Evie sat down with the puppies on her lap. She reached in and pulled the note off and unfolded it. It was one of the messages from the balloons.

At the bottom was some writing.

"Someone wrote another poem!" said Evie. She began to read aloud.

"Had a shoe . . . They bit it!
Had a purse . . . They hid it!
Had a cat . . . They chased it!
Had a postman . . . They raced it!
Have no home for them . . . We're sad!
Found the Pet Patrol . . . We're glad!

Please find good homes for these puppies.
If you can't find homes for them,
I will take them to the dogs' home.
I'll be back to pick them up at 4.00."

The note had been chewed at the corner.

"I can't believe it," said Evie. "The balloons worked!"

Megan didn't answer. She was too busy patting the golden puppies.

Evie's puppies jumped off her lap and ran across the porch.

"Hey, you!" she called, and chased after them.

She gathered the puppies up and looked at the note again. "'Take them to the dogs' home,'" she read. "We *can't* let them go to the dogs' home. Don't worry, puppies," she said to the wiggling balls of fur. "You're with the Pet Patrol now. We'll find homes for you today."

Megan looked up from the golden puppies and nodded her head. "These puppies are *not* going to the dogs' home."

The black puppy in Evie's lap yapped.

Megan and Evie laughed.

"Do you think your mum might let you keep them?" asked Megan.

"Well," said Evie, "remember when I won two goldfish at the autumn fair?"

"Yes," said Megan.

"Mum said, 'Find a home for those fish. Absolutely *no* goldfish in this house.'"

"But you still have Flipper and Goldie," said Megan.

Evie smiled. "Right! And when I brought

32

home Dingo from Brownies camp, Mum said, 'Find a home for that gerbil. Absolutely *no* gerbils in this house.'"

"But you still have Dingo," said Megan.

"Right!" said Evie.

Megan and Evie smiled now.

"And when you brought home Mittens?"

"'Absolutely no cats in this house!'" they said together in an imitation of Evie's mother. They began to laugh.

Evie's mother was a softie when it came to animals.

Evie looked at the puppies.

The brown-and-white one was batting the black one's face like a punch bag. Evie let them roll off her lap on to the porch. Megan put the two golden puppies down, too. The black one crouched down and let out a puppy bark, then pounced on the brown-and-white puppy. The two golden ones jumped on the pile, and the puppy pile rolled over and over.

All four puppies began to yap and bounce across the porch. Evie shook her head and ran to catch them.

"I don't think she'll go for four puppies," said Evie. She frowned. "Besides, I promised her after I brought the two hermit crabs back from the beach that I wouldn't ask for any more pets for a whole year."

Megan looked at Evie and sighed. "That *is* a lot of puppies,' she said. She picked up the note. "Especially when they" – she read again from the note – "bite shoes, hide purses, chase cats, and chase postmen!"

Evie laughed.

"We'd better try something else," Megan said.

Evie lowered the puppies back into the box. They jumped against the sides and yapped. Suddenly they looked like a *lot* of puppies to Evie.

Evie couldn't resist picking up the small black puppy again and rubbing his soft head under her chin. She held him out to look at him. She held him with one thumb under each of his tiny front legs. His small black face looked like a teddy bear's. He licked her finger with a pink tongue.

"Don't get attached to that puppy, Evie," said Megan. "Remember that you can't keep him. You know how you –"

"I won't," said Evie, but she didn't put the black puppy down. She rubbed his head under her chin again.

Megan frowned. She looked at her watch.

"We'd better get busy," she said. "It's twelve o'clock, and we have exactly four hours before they come back to get them. And at four o'clock I —"

She looked at Evie but didn't finish.

"I know," said Evie. "You have to go to Tiffie Sullivan's birthday party."

"Sorry, Evie," said Megan.

"It's OK," said Evie. "I just hope four hours is enough."

Evie's Daydream

"I've got it," said Evie. "A puppy sale!"

"A puppy sale?"

"Yes. Some people have car boot sales. Some people have lemonade sales. We," she added importantly, "are going to have a puppy sale!"

She watched Megan. Megan was thinking.

After a minute, she nodded her head. "Not bad," she said. "Not a bad idea at all. But first we need to get organized."

Evie put the black puppy back in the box with the others. She sat back and listened to Megan plan the sale.

"We need advertising. Signs. I have some poster board at home. We also need a good location for the sale. Your front garden will be perfect. Lots of people walk past here every day. We need a box for the money and . . ."

Evie sat on the top step and rested her chin in her hands. She watched the puppies. She stopped listening to Megan.

". . . a table," Megan continued, "and chairs . . ."

Evie picked up the black puppy again and began to pat him.

"My mum has a small table that we can use," said Megan, "and I have that poster board. You watch the puppies and I'll go and get the stuff."

Megan ran down the steps and across the garden.

"*Puppies for sale!*" she yelled as she ran down the street. "*Puppies for sale!*"

Evie didn't hear Megan. She was scratching the black puppy on his chest. She held a blade of grass over his mouth. He kept trying to grab the grass. Evie smiled at him. She pretended that he was hers. She would be the perfect owner.

She had a fenced-in back garden. She loved animals. She would take him for walks. She would be perfect for him. Except for one thing – her mother. Or rather, her promise to her mother.

Evie let him catch the grass. He took it into his mouth and shook his head back and forth and growled. She looked at the three other puppies, who were sleeping huddled together in a small heap of ears and paws and tails.

If only she could keep them all!

She could just imagine it: Evie's Home for Unwanted Animals.

She would have a big house with a large green garden in front and a field at the back. Somehow in her daydream it looked just like Tiffie Sullivan's house.

Inside, though, it was different. There was no furniture or oriental rugs or breakable vases in the living room. Instead the rooms were filled with dog and cat beds. The dining-room had long rows of bowls. The playroom was filled with balls and sticks and rubber squeaky toys. On a large velvet cushion was the little black puppy.

Or maybe she would keep Tiffie's pink-and-white canopied bed in her daydream for him.

It would be wonderful. Daydreams were always wonderful.

She sighed. "I can't keep you," she said to the puppy.

"*Yap!*" the puppy said. To Evie it sounded like "Yes, you can."

"*Puppies for sale!*" Megan yelled as she came around the corner dragging a small table and a piece of poster board.

Evie put the puppy back in the box and

watched him snuggle down with the others. She ran to help Megan.

They carried the table to the front of Evie's garden and unfolded the legs. Then they put the box on the table. Evie watched the puppies while Megan wrote on the poster board: PUPPIES FOR SALE – £2.00.

Evie looked at the sign. She shook her head. "It needs something," she said. She took the marker and added the words CUTE, ADORABLE, PERFECT, WELL-BEHAVED.

She lifted the marker and started to write again.

"Evie!" said Megan. "Don't you think you're overdoing it?"

"I just need to add one more thing. We can only sell the puppies to good homes, agreed?"

"Agreed."

Evie took the marker and printed on the bottom: ONLY TO GOOD HOMES

"When someone comes up to buy one, you nod if you think they're OK," she said to Megan.

They stood back and looked at the sign. Evie thought for a second.

"Let's put their names on the sign," she said.

"What are their names?" asked Megan. "Did the note have any names?"

"No," said Evie. "We'll have to give them names."

"Well," said Megan. She picked up the two golden puppies. "This one's Ginger, because she's the colour of ginger. This one's Waldo because ... well ... because I like the name Waldo."

"This one will be Spots," Evie said as she picked up the brown-and-white puppy, "because he has spots. And that leaves you," she said to the black puppy.

The black puppy was on his back now, trying to roll back over and stand up. His little round stomach kept getting in the way.

Evie laughed again.

"What's a good name for a little black dog?" she said.

"Blackie," said Megan, "or Shadow."

"No, something special," said Evie.

The black puppy finally got up on his feet. He began to scratch behind his ear. His back foot scratched so hard and fast that he lost his balance and rolled back over in Evie's lap.

"Flea!" said Evie.

Megan stepped back. "Do you think he has fleas?"

"No," said Evie. "His name! I'm going to name him Flea! Flea," she said, holding him up, "meet Ginger, Waldo and Spots. Ginger, Waldo and Spots, meet Flea."

They put the puppies back in the box. Evie took the marker and wrote on the sign: GINGER, WALDO, SPOTS AND FLEA.

"Now," Evie quizzed Megan, "when you see someone coming up to the table and you think that person would have a good home for the puppies, what do you do?"

Megan nodded.

"Yes," said Evie, "like that."

Megan nodded again.

"OK," said Evie, "you've got it. You can stop nodding now."

Megan nodded one more time. She was looking over Evie's shoulder. Evie followed her look.

"Our first customer," Megan said.

Evie took a deep breath and turned round to begin the sale.

Puppies for Sale!

"What's in the box?"

It was Rachel Lewis, pushing a pink plastic doll's pram. She stopped in front of the table and scratched her knee.

"Can't you read?" said Megan, pointing to the sign.

"No," said Rachel. "I'm only four."

Evie lifted the box down from the table. Rachel looked into the box. Her face brightened.

"Oooooo!" she said, her mouth in a perfect circle. "Puppies!"

She grabbed Flea around the neck and began to lift him out of the box.

"Wait!" said Evie, rescuing the puppy. "That's not how you pick up a puppy. Sit down first. And you don't want that little black one, anyway. You want to hold this nice brown-and-white one."

Megan gave Evie a warning look.

"His name is Spots."

"Spots," Rachel repeated.

She sat down on the grass beside the table. Evie carefully picked up Spots under his front legs and put him in Rachel's lap.

When Spots began to lick Rachel's face, she squealed with delight.

She patted him over and over and laughed.

"*Whose* puppies?" she asked.

Evie looked at Megan. Should they or shouldn't they?

Megan nodded.

The Lewises would be a good family for Spots. They didn't have any other pets, and Rachel was being very gentle with Spots.

Evie nodded her approval back to Megan.

"We're selling the puppies for two pounds," Evie said.

"Ooooo!" Rachel's mouth went into a circle again. "Can I buy this puppy?" she asked.

"Sure," said Evie.

Rachel jumped up. She picked up Spots carefully and hugged him. "I'm going home to show my mum," she said. "And get my money."

She lowered him into the doll's pram, where he snuggled down between two stuffed teddy bears and a Smurf. Evie reached down and patted his back.

"Now be very careful with him. OK?"

"OK," said Rachel. She turned the pram and began to push it back towards the Lewises' house.

"Won't Mummy be surprised!" Rachel said as she headed towards home.

Evie looked at Megan.

"Yes she will," Megan said.

They watched Rachel push the doll's pram away, then looked back at the other puppies.

"That was easy enough," said Evie. "One down, three to go."

They put the box back on the table and sat down to wait. Cars drove up and down the street. No one stopped. A few people walked by. They didn't seem interested.

Evie checked her watch. "Someone will come soon," she said. "We'll be through in no time."

"I don't know," said Megan.

"Maybe."

"Maybe not."

"Hey!"

Two boys came towards the table. The taller one bounced a basketball as he walked. *Pong pong pong.*

"Uh-oh," said Evie. It was Matt Morrison. He never went anywhere without his basketball. Joe Bates walked along beside him.

Matt and Joe usually meant trouble.

"Where did you get the puppies?" Matt said. He stooped down beside the box and picked up Waldo.

He began to scratch Waldo under the chin. Waldo's eyes closed.

Joe held out his finger for Flea to chew on.

Evie looked at Megan. Matt and Joe were a little wild. They were always getting into trouble. But . . .

Evie remembered the way Matt had taken care of the class gerbil last summer. And she remembered the pictures that Joe had brought in for his science project on endangered species.

She nodded to Megan. Megan shrugged and nodded back.

"You want one?" said Evie.

"Cool!" said Matt.

"You, too?" she said to Joe.

"Can I pay later?"

Evie thought for a second. She would rather have Matt and Joe take them than send them to

the dogs' home.

"Yes," she said.

"Me, too?" said Matt.

Evie nodded.

Matt smiled. "What's this one's name?" he asked.

"Waldo," said Evie.

Matt put the puppy down and walked a few steps.

"Come on, Waldo," he said. Waldo bounced three steps to catch up with Matt. Matt took another step, and Waldo bounced along three more times. *Step, bounce bounce bounce.*

Joe reached down and picked up Flea.

"Wait a minute," said Evie. "You don't want that one. He's the runt. You want this one." She handed him Ginger.

Megan frowned at Evie.

"OK," said Joe. He took Ginger and put her down. She followed along, too. Off they went across the yard.

"You did it again," Megan said. "Don't get attached to that puppy!"

"Don't be silly," said Evie. "I know I can't keep him. I just thought Ginger would be better for Joe."

"And Spots would be better for Rachel?" said Megan in an accusing voice.

"Yes," said Evie.

Megan looked down at the puppy in the box.

"Well," she said, "he's the only one left. You were right. This is easy."

Evie picked up Flea and rubbed him behind the ears. For once there was no satisfaction in being right.

"Puppies!" a voice squealed from across the street. "I *looove* puppies."

Cassandra Matthews made her way across the street.

Before she even got to the box, Megan was already nodding her approval. They liked Cassandra. She was their favourite babysitter.

"What a sweet thing!" Cassandra said, picking up Flea. "He's a darling. Oh, I've just got to take him home."

Evie couldn't answer. Her throat felt tight.

It was happening too fast. She wasn't ready for Flea to go yet.

Cassandra was holding Flea with one hand. With the other hand she was digging into the pocket of her jeans. She came out with one pound coin and a handful of change.

"Here," she said, dropping the money into the box. "You count it out."

Evie looked at the money in the box where, just a few minutes before, Flea had been. Somehow it didn't seem like a fair exchange.

Megan grabbed the money and counted out a pound from the change. She gave the rest back to Cassandra.

Evie watched as Cassandra walked back down the street talking to Flea.

"Sold!" said Megan.

"Sold," said Evie, but the word had a hollow ring.

Guard Dogs for Sale!

"Look!" said Megan.

Evie looked. A white delivery van drove down Carter's Mill Road. Through the back window of the van they could see dozens of balloons. It was heading towards Tiffie Sullivan's neighbourhood.

Megan smiled. Evie frowned.

Evie had been so excited about the puppies that she had forgotten all about the party.

Megan checked her watch. "We made it in plenty of time for the party!" she said. "We found homes for the puppies in only one hour. Three hours to spare! Now I need to get home and pick out my outfit for the fashion show."

"Great," said Evie, her voice flat.

"Should I wear my lavender pleated skirt with the striped top? Or that hand-painted T-shirt dress?" She began to fold up the table.

Evie didn't answer. She had an empty feeling that she couldn't explain and this time it didn't have anything to do with Tiffie's party. She should feel happy. After all, the puppies now had good homes. And she and Megan had even made a little money.

She sighed and picked up the empty box.

"Let's go take these things back to your house," she said. "I guess I'll help you pick out your outfit."

"Look!" Megan said again. Evie didn't look this time.

"Uh-oh," she heard Megan say.

She looked.

Step, bounce bounce bounce.

Matt and Joe were coming back.

Step, bounce bounce bounce.

Waldo and Ginger trotted happily behind them.

"This doesn't look good," said Megan.

"Maybe they're coming back to pay us."

"No, look at their faces." The boys were frowning.

"You're right. This doesn't look good," said Evie.

"My mum said no," said Matt.

"Mine, too," said Joe. "We have to give them back."

Waldo and Ginger ran over to Megan and

started jumping up on the leg of her jeans. She reached down to pick them up.

"That's OK," she said. She rubbed Waldo's head.

"Sorry," Matt said over his shoulder as he and Joe ran back towards home.

"Now what?" said Megan.

Before Evie could answer, they saw Cassandra coming back from across the street. She wasn't smiling this time.

"I have to give him back," she said. "My parents said no."

Cassandra handed Flea back to Evie. Then she reached out and gave Flea one last pat.

"Sorry," she said to Evie.

"That's all right," said Evie.

She should have been sad, but she wasn't. Flea was back! She scooped up the money from inside the box and handed it to Cassandra.

"Sorry," she said. But when she looked down at Flea she didn't feel one bit sorry.

"Guess we'd better wait for Rachel," said Megan. "She should be along any minute."

"Maybe her mum will let her keep Spots," said Evie.

"No way," said Megan. "They'll all come

back. Just wait and see."

"You don't know for sure," Evie insisted. "Maybe she'll get to keep her."

"Look," said Megan. Coming down the street were Rachel and the pink plastic doll's pram.

"I guess you were right," said Evie.

"Business number six is another failure," said Megan. They were silent as they watched Rachel make her way towards them.

She pushed the pink doll's pram in a zigzag path down the pavement. She took her time, stopping to talk to every bush and tree that she passed.

"Sorry," Evie said when Rachel got close enough to hear her.

"Sorry?" said Rachel. She wheeled the pram up to the table and stopped. "Sorry about what?"

Evie and Megan leaned forward to look into the pram.

"Super!" said Megan.

"Super-duper!" Evie shouted.

Lying in the doll's pram, in between the two teddy bears and the Smurf, were two shiny one-pound coins.

"One down!" said Evie.

"But three to go," said Megan.

The girls sat back down at the table and waited. An hour passed and nothing happened. Cars kept going back and forth on the street and people kept walking past. But no one else had come to buy a puppy.

"The problem," said Megan, "is the sign."

"The problem is not the sign," said Evie. "The problem is that no one wants to buy a puppy."

Megan looked at Evie and spoke slowly. "We need to make people *want* a puppy. Just look at that sign."

Evie looked at the sign. "'Cute, adorable, perfect, well-behaved puppies for sale,'" she read. "What's wrong with that?"

"It's too ordinary."

Megan took down the sign and turned it over. She picked up the marker and wrote: GUARD DOGS FOR SALE.

Evie smiled.

"Let's reduce the price, too," she said.

Megan wrote £1.00 on the bottom of the sign.

They sat back down and waited. Cars drove by. People walked by. Still no one stopped.

Another half an hour passed. Evie checked her watch. "We need a new plan," she said.

They sat in silence for a minute.

"I've got it!"

"Oh, no," said Megan. "You have that look again."

"Wait," said Evie. "This is a great idea. I saw a film once where a baby was left on the doorstep in a basket. When the people came to the door, they saw the baby and right away they wanted to keep him."

"Puppies are not babies," said Megan.

"But it might work, right?"

"Weeell . . ." said Megan.

"We could dress them like babies. They would be irresistible, right?"

"Weeell . . ."

"Do you have a better idea?" said Evie.

Megan thought for a moment, then looked up at Evie.

"Whose house?" she said.

Wee Willie Waldo

"Let's start at the end of Carter's Mill Road and try the first three houses. It'll be great," said Evie. She was already running across the garden to her house. "I'll be right back with the stuff."

Evie ran inside, then came back out carrying a small pile of doll's clothes, a notepad, and three old Easter baskets.

She wrote three notes to go on the baskets:

PLEASE GIVE ME A GOOD HOME.

She taped one note on the top of each basket.

Megan shook her head. She picked up Waldo. She chose a pink nightcap and a striped flannel nightgown to go with last year's pink Easter basket. She began to dress Waldo in the nightgown. Waldo wriggled in her hands. He didn't like the nightgown. Megan finally got him into it and snapped up the back. He tried

to bite the ruffles at the neck. Quickly she tied on the pink nightcap and put him in the basket.

Megan laughed. "He looks like Wee Willie Winkie," she said.

"You mean Wee Willie Waldo!" said Evie.

"We'd better hurry," said Megan. "He won't last long in his clothes."

Evie dressed Ginger. She chose a tiny white bride's dress. Ginger nipped at the veil. Into a white-and-blue basket she went.

Evie looked down. Only Flea was left.

"*Yap!*" he said.

"Maybe we should try those two first," she said.

Megan shook her head. She picked up Flea and stuffed him into a sailor suit. She tied the navy-blue bow beneath his chin and put him in the third basket.

The puppies were all wiggling in their clothes. They were trying to climb out of the baskets.

"This will never work," said Megan.

"Let's just try it," said Evie. "All they have to do is stay in the baskets long enough for the people to get to the door."

They carried the baskets down to the end of the road. The movement of the baskets settled the puppies down.

"I'll take the first two houses," said Evie. "You take the third one. Ring the doorbell and run behind those bushes across the street. We'll meet there."

"OK," said Megan. She headed for the third house.

Evie crept up to the first house.

Gently she put the Easter basket with Waldo in it on the porch. She rang the doorbell and ran to the next house.

There she dropped off Ginger the bride. Again she rang the bell and took off.

She met Megan coming from the third house. They dived behind the bushes and waited.

They couldn't see what was happening. But they heard three doors open. They heard three doors close.

The girls peered over the hedge.

"Can you see?" asked Evie. "Can you see if the baskets are gone?"

Yap!

Around the corner came Wee Willie Waldo. His cap was down under his neck. His nightgown

67

was caught under his legs.

"*Yap!*" he said. His tail wagged happily.

Megan shook her head.

Yap! A small bride puppy came round the corner.

Megan looked at Evie. "This is impossible," she said.

They picked up the puppies. "What about Flea?" said Evie. "Maybe he got adopted."

Yap! Around the corner came Flea. His sailor's bow was untied. He tripped over it as he ran.

Evie sighed. "I don't have any other ideas for now," she said. She began to laugh. She knew she should be cross, but she couldn't be. The puppies looked so funny in their clothes.

"Let's try one more house. Whose house is next?"

"Mrs Hansen?" Evie said.

They had stayed clear of Mrs Hansen since the weed-pulling disaster.

Evie looked at Megan. "It's worth a try," she said. "We can watch from behind her hedge."

They got the baskets back from the first three front porches. Then they straightened Waldo's cap and pulled down his nightgown and put him back in the basket.

69

He yawned. "Good," said Evie. "Maybe he'll go to sleep."

They tiptoed up to Mrs Hansen's front porch. Waldo closed his eyes.

"Perfect," said Evie.

"Perfect," said Megan.

They put the basket down in the front of the door. Megan rang the doorbell. They carried the other puppies and slipped behind the hedge to watch.

No one came to the door.

"Should we ring it again?" asked Evie.

"Shh," said Megan, "here she comes!"

They saw the door open. They saw a hand reach out and take the note from the top of the basket. Then they saw the door close. The basket was left outside on the porch.

Evie looked at Megan. "No go," she said.

Megan and Evie came out from behind the bushes and walked towards Waldo. They carried the other two puppies with them.

Just then the door swung open and Mrs Hansen stepped out.

She was putting her reading glasses on her nose and looking at the note.

"A puppy! Did you girls bring this puppy up

71

here?" she asked. She looked at them over the top of her glasses. It reminded Evie of the way that she had looked at them when they had pulled up her begonias.

Megan and Evie looked down at the pavement.

"Yes," Evie said.

Mrs Hansen looked at the sleeping puppy and back at the children.

"Well," she said, "this won't do. This won't do at all." She looked down again at the puppy.

Evie looked down at her tennis shoes and waited for Mrs Hansen to continue.

"One puppy would be much too lonely here. I would need the little bride, too."

Evie and Megan stood frozen on the path.

"Would that be OK?"

The little bride, too! She wanted *two* puppies!

Evie nudged Megan. Megan stepped forward with Ginger.

"Yes," she said.

Mrs Hansen reached out and took Ginger from Megan.

"Thank you! I have wanted a puppy since my dog Alfie died last year. I just couldn't make myself go and pick one out. Thank you for doing it for me!"

She picked up Waldo. He woke up and his tail began to wag.

"And he doesn't need these clothes, does he?"

Mrs Hansen began to take off the cap and nightgown. "You don't like those clothes, do you?" she said to Waldo. She took off Ginger's bride's dress and veil.

She put the clothes back in the basket and smiled at Evie and Megan. "Come and see them any time," she said. "And come and see me if you girls ever want another job."

"Weeding?" asked Megan in a surprised voice.

"No." Mrs Hansen laughed. "Definitely not weeding! But I may need a puppy-sitter every once in a while."

"Any time!" Evie and Megan said together.

They watched Mrs Hansen as she carried Waldo and Ginger inside. They could hear her talking to the puppies as the door closed.

"You're good little puppies," she was saying. "You want a treat?"

Evie smiled at Megan. "Another good home," she said. "Three down!"

They looked down at Flea. His clothes were

torn and chewed. His tail wagged back and forth.

"*Yap!*" he said.

Megan sighed. "But the hardest one left to go."

A Present for Tiffie

"They'll be coming soon," said Evie.

She walked back down Carter's Mill Road with Megan. She held Flea. He was the only one left now.

She looked at her watch. It was three-thirty.

"They'll be coming to take Flea to the dogs' home in thirty minutes."

"What can we do?" said Megan.

Evie didn't answer. She couldn't. Every time she thought about Flea her throat got tight. She had worried all day about giving Flea to someone else. But at least she had to admit that it would be much easier than sending him to the dogs' home.

"Well," said Megan, "let's think. Who would be a good owner? Let's make a list of things that a dog would like in a home. Then we will ask that person."

"Lots of attention," said Evie.

"A big fenced garden," said Megan.

"Lots of walks," said Evie.

"Someone who likes animals," said Megan.

"I've got it!" said Megan. "I know someone with a big fenced back garden. Who goes for a walk every day. Who would give a dog lots of attention."

Evie smiled.

I *have a big fenced-in back garden*, she thought. I *love pets.* I *would give a dog lots of attention.* I *would take him for walks . . . It must be me!*

"I know just the person," Megan continued. "Tiffie Sullivan."

Tiffie Sullivan!

Evie stopped walking and turned to face Megan.

"Tiffie Sullivan!" she said. "Tiffie Sullivan?"

"Yes," said Megan. "She has a big house and a big fenced-in back garden. She would be perfect. In fact, I'll take Flea over when I go to her party. Flea can be her present!"

Megan smiled. She looked proud of herself. She looked at Evie for approval.

Evie stared at her blankly.

"You can't mean it," she said. "You can't give this dog to Tiffie Sullivan!"

Megan looked at Evie. "Do you want him to go to the dogs' home?"

"No, but . . ."

"Do you have a better idea?"

"No, but . . ."

Megan looked angry. "Name one thing wrong with Tiffie Sullivan and I won't take him."

Evie thought.

The only thing she could think of was that Tiffie wore designer clothes to school. Or rode in a limousine. Or hadn't invited Evie to her birthday party. But none of these was a reason not to have a dog.

Evie looked down at Flea. She rubbed his head under her chin. "You're right," she said. "There's not one thing wrong with Tiffie Sullivan. I have to think of Flea. I have to think of keeping him out of the dogs' home. And if giving him to Tiffie will do that . . . then . . ." She caught her breath. "OK."

She held Flea close and rubbed his soft back one more time, then held him out to Megan. She felt his small wet tongue lick her finger. She blinked.

"Take him," she said. "Go on."

Megan took Flea. She looked at Evie.

"I'm sorry, Evie," she said. "If you could keep him . . ."

The two girls stood for a moment looking at each other without speaking.

"If you *could* keep him . . ."

"I can't."

"I've got to go and get dressed for the party," Megan said. "Do you want to walk over to Tiffie's house with me and help me give her Flea? I'm sure she wouldn't mind."

Evie shook her head. She couldn't speak.

Megan turned and walked away.

Evie watched her walk across the lawn. She watched her walk down Carter's Mill Road and turn out of sight around the corner.

Evie stood staring at the empty street for a moment, then began to walk towards the woods, towards Cooley's Knob.

She wanted to be alone.

The Pet Patrol was finished. She didn't want the responsibility any more. It hurt too much.

The whole idea had been one big mistake.

Cooley's Knob

"Evie, where are you?"

"Not here!"

"Evie!"

"Go away!"

Evie sat at the crest of Cooley's Knob alone. She could hear Megan calling her from the path below.

"Evie!" Megan's voice got louder as she climbed closer and closer to Evie.

"Go away!" called Evie again. She had been sitting for two hours. She didn't want to hear about Tiffie's party and the fashion show and Flea. She wanted to be left alone.

"Evie!" Megan sounded out of breath.

Evie could see her now, panting as she hurried up the path through the woods. She was still dressed for the party. She had worn the lavender skirt.

Evie looked down. She watched a fly land on her shoe. It took off again.

She heard Megan sit down next to her but she didn't look up. She listened to Megan breathing hard beside her.

"Evie," she said, "I went to your house. I couldn't find you anywhere."

Evie looked at Megan. Her friend looked worried.

"I'm sorry," Evie said. "I was sad. Sad about Flea. I came up here to try to forget about it. How did it go? Did you find him a home?"

"Yes," answered Megan. "I found him the best home."

Evie didn't look up or smile.

"He deserves the best home," she said. "Tiffie was very happy, I'm sure."

"Tiffie's mother said no," said Megan.

"She did?" said Evie.

"Yeah. Flea jumped on Mrs Sullivan's leg and tore her tights."

"No!" Evie said. She covered her mouth with her hand. "He didn't!"

"Yes," said Megan, nodding her head, "he did. Then he jumped up on Tiffie's lap and made paw prints on her white designer dress."

"No!" said Evie again. "He didn't!"

"Yes, he did. That's not all. He barked during

the fashion show and chewed on Mr Sullivan's tasselled shoes."

"No!" said Evie. When she thought of Flea chewing the shoes she began to giggle.

"Then he played hide-and-seek with one of Tiffie's birthday presents."

"No!" said Evie again.

"Yes!" said Megan. They were both laughing now.

"And remember the oriental rug in their hall that I told you about, the one that came all the way from India? The one that no one is allowed to walk on? Well, I guess Flea really *had* to . . ."

"He didn't!" said Evie.

"He did!" Megan said. "We were evicted from the party."

Evie's smile was gone. "I'm sorry," she said.

"It's OK," said Megan. "I'm not sorry. I guess it wouldn't have been such a good home for him after all."

"No, it wouldn't have," agreed Evie.

She wondered who had taken Flea. Somehow she didn't want to know the answer. As long as she didn't know who had him, she wouldn't have to think about herself not having him.

"So," said Megan. "We have a new member

of the Pet Patrol."

Evie looked up quickly. After all that had happened, she couldn't believe that Megan had asked Tiffie to join the Pet Patrol.

"Tiffie?" she asked.

Megan laughed.

"No," she said. "Tiffie doesn't even like animals. Tiffie's mum said no, but *your* mum said yes!"

They heard a yap from the path below. Around the corner, hurrying on his short stubby legs, came Flea. His tiny tongue was hanging out as he ran towards the girls. It had been a long trip up the path behind Megan.

"Come on, slow coach," said Megan. But Evie didn't hear her. She was running down the path towards Flea.

She whisked him up into her arms and carried him the rest of the way up the hill. She rubbed his head under her chin and kissed his ears. He licked her finger. Suddenly her eyes filled with tears.

"My mum really said yes?" she asked.

Megan smiled and nodded her head.

"I promised I wouldn't ask her," said Evie.

"But *you* didn't," said Megan. "I did. When I

went to your house to find you I told her all about it. She said yes."

"My mum said yes!" Evie said again and again. If she said it enough, she might begin to believe that it was true.

"My mum said yes!" she said to Flea.

"*Yap!*" said Flea.

Evie held Flea close for a moment. Then she looked up at Megan. "Did the people come back for the puppies?" she asked.

"Not before I left," said Megan. "But I left them a note." She pulled a folded sheet of notebook paper out of her pocket. "I copied it for you." She handed it to Evie.

Evie took the sheet of paper from Megan, unfolded it, and began to read it out loud.

"Puppy no. 1 . . . We had a sale!
Puppy no. 2 . . . We did not fail!
Puppy no. 3 . . . We found a way!
Puppy no. 4 . . . He's ours to stay!"

Evie hugged Megan. Megan hugged Evie. And together they hugged the newest member of the Pet Patrol.

Just Wait

"There are nine more balloons out there somewhere," said Evie.

Evie, Megan, and Flea stood together at the crest of Cooley's Knob. They were looking south towards Douglasville, Minnistron, Six Mile, and Grumptown.

"Right now someone could be reading the message. Now someone could be on their way to my house to find —"

"No way," said Megan.

"It might work," said Evie. "It worked once. It could work again."

"Don't get your hopes up," said Megan.

Evie stared out at the blue sky. The memory of the orange balloons was clear in her mind. She could remember the cluster breaking apart, each balloon travelling in its own direction, each carrying its message. She thought about the one that had already landed. That one had brought them Spots and Ginger and Waldo and Flea.

She smiled as she thought of Spots being pushed in the doll's pram, of Ginger and Waldo in Mrs Hansen's arms, and of Flea with them on Cooley's Knob.

'It will work," she said. "It will work. Just wait."

The Pet Patrol sat in silence for a few minutes. Then they took one more look at the sky and turned to walk down the mountain.

WILD THINGS
Pet Patrol 2
Betsy Duffey

Someone or something is raiding the dustbin at night. Matt and Joe, known as the wild things, unfairly blame Evie's dog Flea. Evie and Megan are determined to prove them wrong, and solve the mystery. Can the pet patrol crack the case?

This is the second exciting adventure featuring the pet patrol – a must for all animal lovers!

ANIMAL RESCUE
Pet Patrol 3
Betsy Duffey

A stray cat, dog and rabbit need urgent help. Unless Evie and Megan can find new homes for them, these abandoned pets are due to be put to sleep. Plan 1 – to reunite them with their owners fails. But Evie and Megan come up with a brilliant Plan Two. You can be sure the pet patrol won't let them down!

A third exciting adventure featuring the pet patrol – a must for all animal lovers.

BEETHOVEN'S SECOND
Robert Tine

The Newton family are quite happy as dog people. But never in a million years did George Newton think they would be puppy people.

Enter Beethoven, followed by his friend, Missy, and their four St Bernard puppies. They are cuter than cute and messier than anything. None the less, just like Beethoven, George and his family quickly grow to love them all.

It's a big thing to look after so many dogs. It's an even bigger thing when there are nasty people around who want to put the puppies into breeding kennels, which means it's down to Beethoven and George to save the day!

WOOF! THE NEVER ENDING TALE
Terrance Dicks

Rex Thomas is a boy. Rex Thomas is a dog.

The thing is, he can change between the two at any time. One minute he's lying in bed, the next he's sniffing around his bedroom as a small shaggy mongrel with large brown eyes. Fortunately for Rex, his best friend Michael Tully can help him get out of the stickiest of situations.

Even so, when some 'dog therapy' is required for the local milkman, who better to use than Rex, and when Great Demento the Magician loses his canine assistant Cyril, there's only one dog who can take his place. Life for Rex the boy is always eventful — life for the dog is always an adventure.